A Fun Story About Allergy and Asthma Triggers

Published by
JayJo Books, LLC
P.O. Box 213
Valley Park, MO 63088-0213

Edited by Barbara A. Mitchell

Library of Congress Cataloging-in-Publication Data
Gosselin, Kim
ZooAllergy/Kim Gosselin – First Edition
Library of Congress Catalog Card Number 96-76349
1. Juvenile/Fiction/Health Related

ISBN 0-9639449-4-0
Library of Congress

*Proud publishers of the *Special Kids in School*® series written to educate peers of children living with chronic conditions and/or special needs.

> *This book is dedicated to all children*
> *living with allergies and asthma,*
> *and to Gary, Jayson and Justin.*

IF YOU HAVE ASTHMA, JOIN OUR CLUB!

A UNIQUE CLUB
FOR CHILDREN WITH ASTHMA

Asthma Explorers is an educational program sponsored by Fisons Corporation, a Rhône-Poulenc Rorer company.
ASTHMA EXPLORERS is a registered service mark of Fisons Corporation.

The publication of **ZooAllergy** was made possible through a generous Educational Grant by Rhône-Poulenc Rorer Pharmaceuticals Inc.

*The opinions expressed in **ZooAllergy** are those solely of the author. Allergy and asthma care are highly individualized. One should **never** alter allergy or asthma care without first consulting a member of the individual's professional medical team.

Today was Justin's second appointment with Dr. Casey, the allergy "specialist." On his first visit, she listened to his lungs, looked in his nose and throat, checked his ears and eyes, and asked him a LOT of questions!

On this visit he was back for "skin testing." He wasn't exactly sure what that meant, but he knew it had something to do with his allergies. He glanced at his reflection in the mirror. His under-eye circles looked darker than usual, and a reddish-colored crease seemed forever etched across the bridge of his nose.

"Why is it so important to know what I'm allergic to?" he asked his mother, rubbing his nose with the palm of his hand. "I want to go to the zoo NOW!" he said.

"I promised you a trip to the zoo right after your allergy appointment," answered his mother gently, but firmly. "You want to feel better, don't you?"

"Good morning, Justin," Dr. Casey's nurse said, with a smile in her voice. "My name is Karen, and I'm going to help with your allergy testing. Everything we need is right here on this tray. Want to take a closer look?"

Justin squirmed on the examining table and peered over the tray. "What's that weird-looking thing?" Justin asked, pointing to the "creature-like" object lying among the cotton balls, bottles, and alcohol swabs.

"That's what I'm going to be testing you with," Karen giggled. "Now, let's get your shirt off. I need to get your back extra clean," she said, squirting some reddish-brown stuff from the tall bottle on the tray.

"That's cold!" Justin exclaimed.

"I know, but try to hold still," Karen said, as she showed him how it would feel with a gentle poke of the testing "tool."

"It doesn't hurt!" Justin exclaimed with relief.

Karen wrote numbers on his back with a black washable marking pen and drew little squares around the pin-pricks she had made. Justin's mom smiled and told him it looked like a "dot-to-dot" puzzle game.

"It tickles," he giggled aloud.

"You did just GREAT," Karen told him with a reassuring smile. "Be careful not to scratch," she called, swinging the door behind her.

A few minutes later Dr. Casey peeked around the corner of the door. "Hi! Remember me?" she asked, inspecting Justin's back. "The magic is happening," she added, motioning for Justin's mom to come and take a look.

Justin's mom saw a lot of little red bumps! "My gosh!" she exclaimed, "Your back is just covered in little red bumps!"

"Little red bumps?!?!" Justin asked, horrified. "What do they mean?"

"Everything will be fine," answered Dr. Casey, patting Justin's hand. "The little red bumps are going to tell us what you could be allergic to."

"Can I still go to the zoo today like we've planned?"

"The ZOO? Why, of course you can," replied the doctor. "In fact, I'm going to have you try some new medicine while you're here, and I bet you'll begin to feel much, much better."

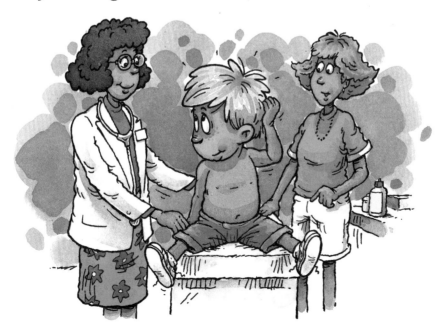

Justin's mom followed the doctor out the door and asked one of the nurses for a small hand mirror. She brought it back and held it at just the perfect angle.

Finally Justin was able to see what all the commotion was about!

"Wow! My back sure looks funny," he grinned. "You don't think I'm getting the chicken pox again, do you Mom?"

"No!" she laughed, tousling his thick wavy hair.

It wasn't long before Karen and Dr. Casey came back for a final look.

"I see several things you're probably allergic to," the doctor said, looking over her notes. "Mold is one of your biggest culprits."

"You mean like the gross green stuff that grows on the old cheese my mom forgets in the refrigerator?"

"Kind of," answered the doctor, smiling. "Only this mold tends to grow more outdoors, especially during damp and rainy weather."

"Let's see . . .," she went on. "It looks like you're also allergic to dust mites, tree pollen, animal fur and dander. Did you tell me once before that you had a pet at home?"

"Yeah, I have a turtle named Speedster," answered Justin, proudly. "What's dander, Dr. Casey?"

"Dander is the animal's dry and flaky skin. It lies underneath their fur and can trigger allergies."

"Can I keep Speedster?" Justin asked, worriedly.

"Sure," replied the doctor, "unless he starts growing a fur coat! But because of your mold allergy, try to keep Speedster's home out of your bedroom, okay?"

Dr. Casey then handed Justin's mother some sheets of blue paper with typewritten words and drawings on them. The doctor talked softly. Justin heard her mention "turning on the air conditioning," "removing stuffed animals," and "putting in tile or wooden floors instead of carpeting (especially in his bedroom)."

Dr. Casey showed Justin how to carefully measure his new medicine (liquid and pills), and how to correctly use his nasal spray. She explained that, in the future, he might need to get allergy shots (like some of his friends did). But, for now, they would try the new medications instead.

"I'll need to see you in a few weeks," she said, "just to make sure everything is going well. Have fun at the zoo!"

PFSSST!...

Justin's mom got in her car and immediately rolled up all the windows and turned the air conditioning on. Already she was taking Dr. Casey's good advice. Mold and tree pollen could stay outdoors where they belonged!

"I'm sure glad that's all over, Mom, even if it didn't hurt very much. Now we can have some fun!"

"Hey! This isn't the way to the zoo," he remarked, glancing out the side window.

"It isn't? Maybe that's because I promised your friend Ashley we'd pick her up along the way."

"You DID!?" Justin exclaimed, practically flying off the front seat.

"I sure did," she answered, putting her arm around him. "I called her grandmother last night to ask her permission."

It wasn't long before they reached Ashley's grandmother's house. Once Ashley was in the car, the two chatted away about Justin's trip to Dr. Casey's office. They "compared" allergies, talked about medicine, and showed each other their asthma inhalers.

"I'm allergic to tree pollen, too," Ashley informed him.

"You are? Anything else?"

"Yeah, straw, hay, and dust mites," she replied. "They make me start coughing like crazy. Sometimes I end up having an asthma episode. Taking my allergy medicine helps, but it doesn't always stop them from happening altogether."

"Make sure you both have your medicine and inhalers before you get out of the car," Justin's mother told them, as she pulled the car into a parking place.

"Hey, Mom!" Justin said, hopping out and reaching for his backpack. "I've got a great idea! Let's make up a game while we're at the zoo. It can be about allergies!"

"An allergy game?" she asked.

"Sure," exclaimed Ashley, her eyes brimming with excitement. "We'll call it ZOOALLERGY!"

Justin's mom began to laugh. "You're on," she said, locking the car doors. "Let's go see how many ZOOALLERGY triggers we can discover today!"

"Wow! Look at all the flowering trees!" exclaimed Ashley.

"Oh! They're beautiful!" said Justin's mother. "But I think we've just found our first allergy trigger."

"Tree POLLEN!" shouted Justin.

"Oooops," Ashley interrupted, stifling a sneeze. "I forgot to take my allergy medicine this morning," she said, reaching into her hip pocket for her nasal spray.

The three explorers soaked up the sunshine and strolled towards the first animal display. Two giraffes, arching their long, long necks, were nibbling leaves from the top of an old, old tree.

"Can you be allergic to giraffes?" asked Ashley.

"I don't really know for sure," answered Justin's mom. "But they do have fur and maybe dander, so I guess it's possible."

"That's three allergy triggers: POLLEN, FUR, and DANDER," announced Justin, skipping on ahead. "Let's go," he called back.

The two had to run extra fast to catch up with Justin. He was already visiting the next animal display and this one was his very favorite!

The hustle and bustle inside the elephant house had an extra aura of excitement. It was Zinder's first birthday! She was the zoo's most famous baby elephant. They arrived just in time to see her kick her birthday cake playfully with one of her massive feet.

"She's soooo cute," cooed Ashley to Justin.

"She sure is," Justin replied. "And no allergy triggers here, right Mom? Elephants don't have any fur."

"That's true," answered Justin's mother. "But remember, kids can still be allergic to animals without fur. And look over there in the corner."

"HAY!" Ashley wailed. "Our fourth allergy trigger."

Soon Ashley, Justin and his mother stopped to take a break on one of the zoo's many wooden benches. A beautiful peacock strutted by, proudly fanning his colorful tail feathers for all to admire.

"Look at that," squealed Ashley. "Aren't they the prettiest feathers you've ever seen?"

"They're AWESOME!" Justin exclaimed.

"They're also allergy triggers," stated his mother, munching on a pretzel. "Remember, a lot of kids are allergic to feathers as well as animal fur."

"Well that's our fifth trigger. Let's get going and find the next one," Justin said, skipping ahead as usual.

"What kind of animal is that?" Ashley inquired. "He's HUGE!"

"He sure is," answered Justin's mother. "He's called a rhinoceros, and he comes from Africa."

Seconds later, the mighty white rhino stomped his feet, stirring up a mighty thunder cloud of dust. Justin and Ashley backed away from the fence, covering their mouths as they coughed and began to wheeze.

"DUST! I guess we've found our sixth trigger," choked Ashley.

"Well, this dust isn't the same as house dust caused by dust mites," interrupted Justin's mother. "But something in the air is definitely a trigger, so let's go ahead and count DUST!"

Rushing over to a nearby concession stand, Ashley and Justin stopped to use the inhalers that would help their asthma symptoms, while Justin's mom purchased ice cold drinks. She was tempted to order a bag of freshly roasted peanuts too, but passed when she remembered that Ashley was allergic to them.

"CERTAIN KINDS OF FOODS!" she called out to the two of them! Their seventh allergy trigger!!

"See how some allergies can trigger asthma episodes?" she asked, referring to that nasty dust cloud the rhino had kicked up a few minutes before.

"Good thing we were prepared," added Ashley, slipping her asthma relief inhaler back into her pocket.

It wasn't long before Ashley and Justin felt much, much better. Soon they found themselves at the foot of an old stone building covered in dark green ivy. The sign on the post read REPTILE HOUSE.

"Let's go in," said Justin's mom. "It will be nice and cool inside."

Justin's mother was right! The large open rooms felt nice and cool.

An alligator gazed at them lazily from his private pond below. Two turtles poked their heads out from permanent shell homes, and a sandy-colored snake slept on a rock nearby.

Justin's mom pointed out several areas where their eighth allergy trigger, MOLD, could be growing. The alligator's pond, different animal cages, and the rain-forest atmosphere all lent themselves to the growing of mold.

Suddenly, from a corner of the room, a zookeeper brought out a small wooden box with tiny holes on top. He opened the box, and gently lifted out a green baby lizard with bright yellow stripes.

"Would you like to pet it?" the zookeeper asked.

"I would! I would!" Ashley screamed.

"Very gently," said the zookeeper, carefully cradling the tiny baby lizard in his large, rough hands.

Ashley gingerly stroked the baby lizard's back, gazing at it with adoration.

"I think you've made a new friend," whispered Justin.

"I think so too," whispered Ashley. "And this one might not have any allergy triggers . . . at least, there's no fur or feathers."

Justin's mother came up from behind, giving them both a hug. The day had suddenly slipped away all too fast as twilight made its first appearance from the windows above.

"Who's ready for a nice, relaxing ride on the zoo's famous train?" she asked.

"ALL AAAABOARD," yelled the conductor, ringing the bright red engine's shiny brass bell.

Justin and Ashley grasped hands and giggled in unison as they climbed aboard the train.

"Well, kids, how many allergy triggers did we discover today?"

"Eight all together," Ashley responded proudly, "if we count the rhino's DUST."

"I think you're right," said Justin. "Let's see . . . TREE POLLEN, ANIMAL FUR, DANDER, FEATHERS, HAY, DUST, CERTAIN KINDS OF FOODS, and MOLD," he counted. "Can we come back and play ZOOALLERGY again soon, Mom?"

"Can we pleeease?" begged Ashley.

The conductor clanged the shiny brass bell one last time before chugging along. Thick black smoke rose from the smokestack as Justin's mother rested her head against the wooden frame of her bench.

In front of her, Ashley and Justin sat snuggled in their seats. Their minds wandered freely over all the ZOOALLERGY discoveries they'd made that day – from Justin's morning visit with Dr. Casey all the way to the adorable new friend Ashley had made in the reptile house.

The End

Justin and Ashley discovered EIGHT different allergy triggers while visiting the zoo. Can you find them? Good luck and have lots of fun!!

How well did you do? Try visiting the zoo with your family, or suggest a school field trip. See how many different ZOOALLERGY triggers YOU can discover!!

To order additional copies of **ZooAllergy** contact your local bookstore or library. Or call the publisher directly at (314) 861-1331 or (800) 801-0159. Write to us at:

JayJo Books, LLC
P.O. Box 213
Valley Park, MO 63088-0213

Ask about our special quantity discounts for schools, hospitals, and affiliated organizations. Fax us at 314-861-2411.

Look for other books by Kim Gosselin including:

Taking Diabetes to School

Taking Asthma to School

Taking Seizure Disorders to School

Taking Asthma to Camp
(A Fictional Story About Asthma Camp)

. . . and new titles coming soon!

A portion of the proceeds from all our publications are donated to various charities to help fund important medical research and education.

We work hard to make a difference in the lives of children with chronic conditions and/or special needs. ***Thank you for your support.***

Ask about future books in our ***"Special Kids in School"*** ® series!